Hey Diddle Diddle

Hey Diddle

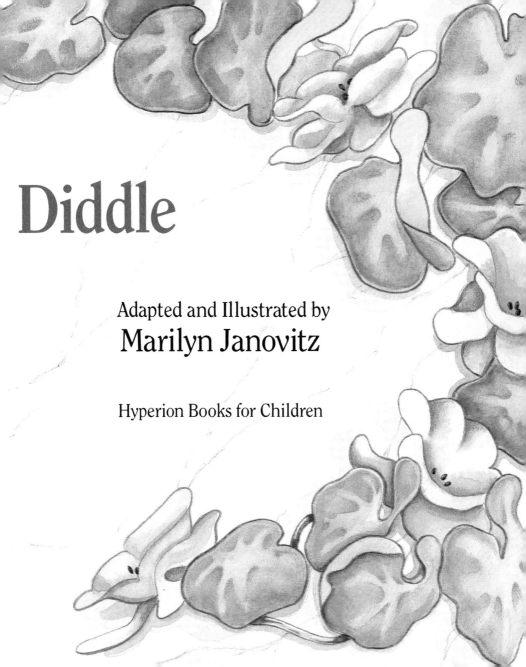

Diddle

Adapted and Illustrated by
Marilyn Janovitz

Hyperion Books for Children

For Lydia

Text and illustrations copyright © 1992 by Marilyn Janovitz.
All rights reserved. Printed in the United States of America.
For information address Hyperion Books for Children,
114 Fifth Avenue, New York, New York 10011.

First Edition
1 3 5 7 9 10 8 6 4 2

Library of Congress Cataloging-in-Publication Data
Janovitz, Marilyn.
Hey diddle diddle / adapted and illustrated
by Marilyn Janovitz — 1st ed.
p.   cm.
Summary: An illustrated version of the traditional nursery rhyme.
ISBN 1-56282-168-7 (trade) — ISBN 1-56282-169-5 (lib. bdg.)
1. Nursery rhymes.   2. Children's poetry.   [1. Nursery rhymes.]
I. Title.
PZ8.3.J263He   1992   398.8—dc20   91-26483   CIP   AC

The artwork for each picture consists of watercolor and colored pencil
and is prepared on Arches watercolor paper.

This book is set in 24-point ITC Clearface.

Hey diddle

diddle,

the cat and

the fiddle,

the cow jumped

over the moon.

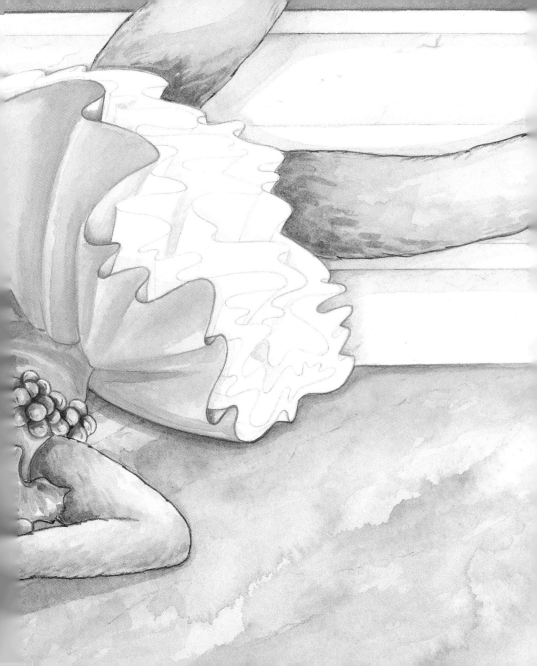

The little dog laughed

to see such a sight,

and the dish ran away

with the spoon.

Hey Did-dle Did-dle, The cat and the fid-dle, The

cow jumped o - ver the moon; ____ The

lit-tle dog laughed to see such a sight And the

dish ran a - way with the spoon.

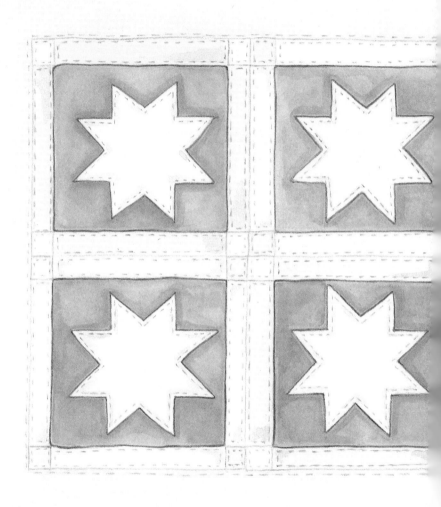